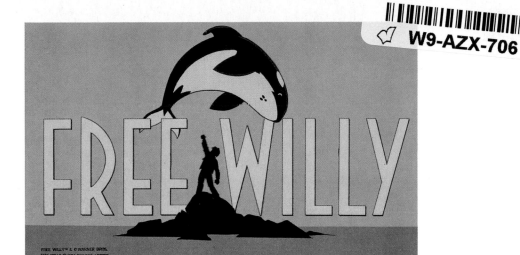

FREE WILLY™ & © WARNER BROS.
FREE WILLY © 1994 NELVANA LIMITED

THE EEL BEAST

BASED ON EPISODES OF THE NEW ANIMATED SERIES
FROM WARNER BROS.

ADAPTED BY CAROL THOMPSON
ILLUSTRATED BY JOSIE YEE

FAMILY ENTERTAINMENT

READING

SCHOLASTIC INC.

New York   Toronto   London   Auckland   Sydney

ISBN 0-590-25962-8

Copyright © 1996 by Warner Bros. Inc.
All rights reserved. Published by Scholastic Inc. by arrangement with Warner Bros. Inc.
Free Willy, characters, names, and all related indicia are trademarks of Warner Bros. © 1996 Warner Bros. Productions, Ltd., Monarchy Enterprises B.V., Le Studio Canal +.

12 11 10 9 8 7 6 5 4 3 2   6 7 8 9/9 0 1/0

Printed in the U.S.A.   24

First Scholastic printing, April 1996

"There's a high fly fish into de-e-e-p center field," called Jesse in his sports announcer voice. "Willy goes back. He leaps. He makes the catch!"

Willy landed in the Healing Pond with a thunderous splash, soaking Jesse from head to toe. "Hey–!" cried Jesse. Just then Randolph hurried outside.

3

Randolph was the manager of the Misty Island Oceanographic Institute, where Jesse worked after school. Jesse loved the ocean. After all, his best pal was a killer whale.

"Where's Marlene?" asked Randolph, looking for the institute's young marine specialist.

Jesse shrugged. "She took Einstein for a swim."

"Swimming with a dolphin isn't like swimming with Willy," said Randolph, raising a pair of binoculars to his eyes. "Willy can help if something goes wrong. *Uh-oh!*"

Marlene and Einstein were being chased by two killer whales!

Randolph and Jesse jumped into the speedboat and bounced across the waves toward Marlene. When the two orcas heard the sound of the motor, they turned and headed out to sea.

Marlene was shivering as Jesse helped her aboard.

"It's all right, Marlene. They're gone," said Randolph soothingly. "But you should always take along a reliable swimming partner when you go out."

Beside the boat, Einstein made happy dolphin squeaks.
"Oh, Einstein, you were so brave!" exclaimed Marlene.
"Killer whales don't scare you!"
Suddenly Willy popped up next to Marlene with a spout
blast.

"*Aaaah!*" screamed Marlene.

"Hey, it's okay," said Jesse. "It's just Willy."

Willy made some friendly squeaks and Marlene sighed. "Sorry, Willy. Some of your relatives invited me to lunch, and I'm feeling a little jumpy."

"I've never heard of orcas attacking humans or dolphins," Randolph said. "I'm sure the orcas were just being playful."

Willy and Einstein watched as the boat sped back to the institute. "I wish we could understand Marlene the way we understand Jesse," Willy told Einstein. "Why was she so upset?"

"Well," Einstein replied. "She thinks two killer whales just tried to eat her."

"No way, little brother!" cried Willy.

"I know," answered Einstein. "But right now, Marlene is scared of killer whales – including you!"

That night a dark form swam silently past the dock outside Jesse's house. It surfaced and spat a stream of water at Jesse's bedroom window. *BLAT-A-TAT-TAT!*

Jesse opened the window – just in time to get sprayed right in the face. "Willy!" he sputtered. "I can't go out this late!" But Willy had something to show him.

Jesse looked down and saw that he was soaked. "Oh, well," he said with a laugh. "I'm already wet!"

Willy raced across the moonlit sea with Jesse on his back. "If my parents find out I split in the middle of the night, I'll probably get grounded." Jesse checked his air gauge. "We can't stay too long," he said. "I only have an hour of air."

"No problem," said Willy, diving smoothly beneath the surface.

"There's the stuff I was telling you about," said Willy, swimming toward a brightly glowing mass of phosphorescent plankton.

"Cool," Jesse replied. "What is that gunk?"

"Don't know," answered Willy. "You'll have to ask Marlene—she's not speaking to me."

"Aw, don't worry, big guy," said Jesse. "She just needs some time to get over what happened today."

Suddenly Jesse pointed toward the ocean floor. "Look!"
His diving light was shining on the colossal crater of an
extinct volcano.

"Yeah, it's a beauty," said Willy.

As they swam closer, Jesse could see that the floor of
the volcano was full of many smaller craters. What he
couldn't see was a pair of giant eyes that glared at him
from the dark depths of a nearby crater.

Jesse decided to play a trick on Willy. He switched off his diving light and ducked into a crater. Within seconds, Willy had spotted him. "Jesse, it's dangerous to goof around in there," said Willy.

"Come on," teased Jesse. "You sound like somebody's parents."

Suddenly Willy cried out in a frightened voice, "Jesse! Behind you!"

"Oh, right," said Jesse. "Like I'm going to fall for that old—huh?!"

Jesse felt something bump into him. He looked around and saw a monster eel with glowing eyes!

CLANK! Before Jesse could swim away, the beast clamped its teeth onto Jesse's scuba tanks and dragged him down into the tunnel.

"Aaah! Willy, help!" screamed Jesse.

Willy howled and slammed his huge body against the crater opening. But he couldn't fit inside. Willy turned and sped off to the surface.

Marlene was at the Healing Pond late that night, checking on Einstein. Suddenly, Willy burst out of the water and started splashing wildly.

Marlene was frightened by the excited killer whale. "Jesse isn't here, Willy," she cried. "He's home in bed."

Again and again, Willy raced out to the inlet, then back to shore, squeaking frantically. "I don't like this," said Marlene. She decided to call Jesse's foster parents, Annie and Glen Greenwood. Then she called Randolph.

"Jesse isn't in his room," she told Randolph. "His diving gear is gone."

"Yesterday Jesse only had about an hour of air left," said Randolph anxiously. "It'll take me too long to get to the institute."

Randolph could hear Willy's worried squeaks in the background. "Willy will go with you."

"That's what I'm afraid of," said Marlene. But she had to find Jesse.

Meanwhile, the giant eel had pulled Jesse deep into the dark tunnels under the ancient volcano. "Let me go, you creep!" cried Jesse.

The creature threw Jesse against a wall. *GRRR!* The Eel Beast's white fangs glistened in the dim light. Jesse held his breath as its fierce, neon eyes glided closer and closer.

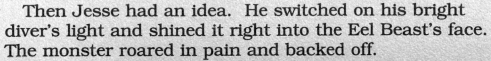

Then Jesse had an idea. He switched on his bright diver's light and shined it right into the Eel Beast's face. The monster roared in pain and backed off.

Now's my chance, thought Jesse, swimming away as fast as he could. Behind him, two angry, glowing eyes blinked open. Silently the creature followed Jesse down the passageway.

Willy's spectacular swimming leaps guided Marlene's boat into the open sea. Even at high speed, the boat could barely keep up.

Soon Willy dived, and Marlene brought the boat to a stop. She put on her gear and followed Willy into the dark sea. Her heart was pounding. *Here I am*, thought Marlene, *diving alone . . . at night . . . with a killer whale!*

Meanwhile, Jesse swam along desperately, lost in the maze of tunnels. Suddenly two glowing eyes appeared in the darkness ahead. Jesse gasped and plastered himself against the side of the tunnel. A big, weird fish glided by, and Jesse breathed a sigh of relief.

He checked his air gauge. Not much time left. Then Jesse heard the distant echo of Willy's woeful whale song. He raced on—determined to find a way out.

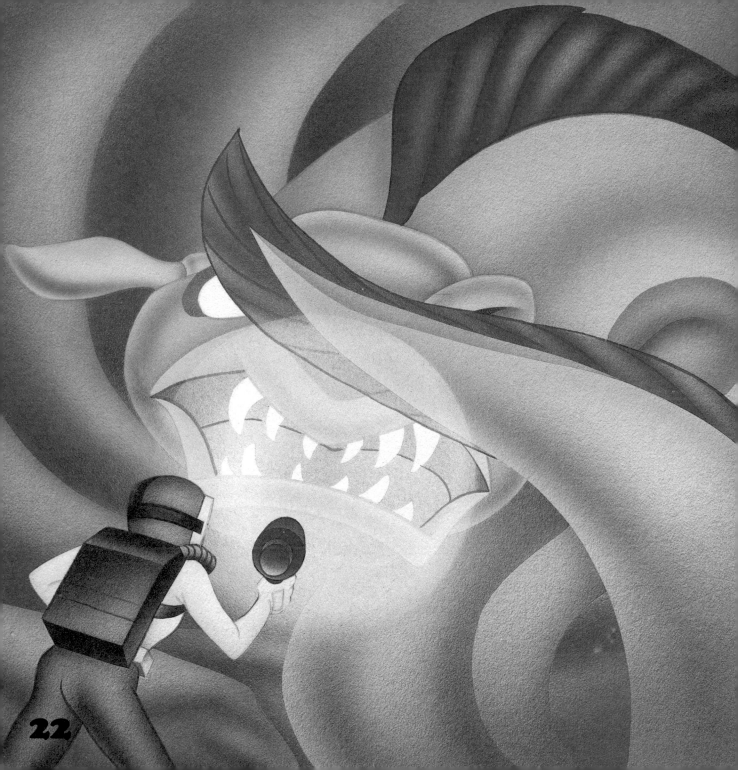

Instead of a way out, Jesse found the Eel Beast! Terrified, he aimed his light at the creature. But it just crept closer, using its tail to shield its eyes.

"Look," Jesse said nervously, turning his light toward the ceiling. "There's a way we can talk." He closed his eyes, calmed himself, and tried to focus. "Can-you-un-der-stand-me?" he asked.

The beast roared angrily. "I hear you. But how?"

"I'm a Truth Talker," Jesse explained. "I can talk to, well . . . animals."

"Yes, I am an animal and proud of it!" snarled the Eel Beast. "You evil grounders intrude on our world with your noises and poisons . . . and *lights!*"

With that, the giant eel lunged at Jesse and crushed his diver's light. In the darkness, Jesse felt the beast's powerful tail circling his body.

Then a bright light flared in the tunnel. It was Marlene!

Marlene tossed an underwater torch at the Eel Beast,
and the creature fled down the tunnel. "Come on, rookie!"
Marlene called to Jesse.

"Ha-haa! You found me!" cried Jesse, swimming after her.

"Thanks to your pal, Willy," said Marlene. Suddenly the tunnel opened into a vast cavern where a shipwreck lay on the ocean floor.

"Radioactive waste," said Marlene, pointing to the barrels. "It must have been down here a long time. That explains some of the weird fish in the tunnels—and the size of that eel."

"Good thing the institute's special diving suits protect us," said Jesse.

Marlene looked up. "Looks like we're in the cone of an extinct volcano. There's our exit." As Jesse and Marlene began to swim to the surface, a savage roar filled the cavern.

"It's the beast!" shouted Jesse. "Swim for it!"

Jesse and Marlene swam as hard as they could, but the Eel Beast gained on them. Its horrifying roar became louder and louder, drowning out all other sounds— except the howl of an angry killer whale!

"It's Willy!" cried Jesse. "Whooa!" He and Marlene were tossed and tumbled in Willy's wake as he zoomed by.

KA-BASH! Willy hit the Eel Beast head-on, knocking it backward. The monster eel crashed to the cavern floor and slipped into a crater too small for Willy to enter.

With a fierce bellow, Willy rammed into the crater once, twice, three times. A low rumble rose from the depths of the cavern. Cracks formed in the walls. Chunks of rock began to fall, and Willy took off for the surface.

Jesse and Marlene cleared the rim of the crater as it began to crumble.

"Where's Willy?" asked Marlene, worried.

WHOOSH! Willy darted out of the opening just in time. The entire ceiling of the cavern came crashing down, burying the radioactive waste forever.

The three friends headed for the surface. But suddenly Jesse found himself gasping. "I'm out of air!" he choked.

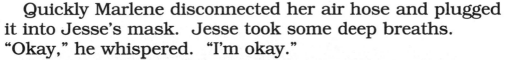

Quickly Marlene disconnected her air hose and plugged it into Jesse's mask. Jesse took some deep breaths. "Okay," he whispered. "I'm okay."

"Let's go home, rookie," Marlene said with a smile.

As the divers reached the surface, two glowing eyes peered at them from far below. "Stay out of my domain, grounders," sneered the Eel Beast. "Stay away from the sea!"

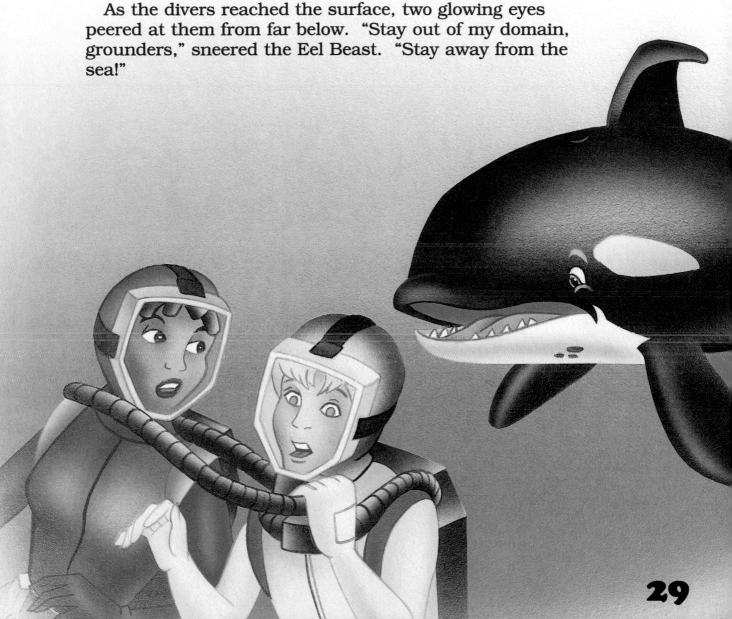

29

As Marlene pulled the speedboat into the institute's boathouse, Jesse saw his foster parents waiting with Randolph on the docks.

Glen tousled the boy's hair and said, "Anytime you go somewhere, you're supposed to leave a note, mister."

Jesse nodded and apologized. "Next time I take off, I'll definitely let someone know where I'm going!"

The next morning Jesse found Marlene at the Healing Pond. "You okay?" he asked.

"Sure," said Marlene with a grin. "I'm just glad we checked out clean on the radioactivity test."

"Yeah," agreed Jesse. "I've been thinking. That monster eel was created by human carelessness."

"True," Marlene said. "But there's still time for us to clean up our act."

"Right." Jesse nodded. With a twinkle in his eye he added, "And there's still time for you to go for a ride—on Willy!"

Marlene laughed. "No way. Willy and I are getting to be friends again, but for now I'll stick to speedboats!" She reached out and gingerly patted the big orca, who squeaked happily.

Then Willy glided across the pond, flew out of the water in a majestic leap, and sped out to sea for a nice long swim.